Richard Scarry's
STORYTIME

CARNIVAL

A SUMMER PICNIC

t was a bright, sunny summer day.
here was not a cloud in the sky.

iss Honey and her boyfriend, Bruno,
ecided to take all the children on a pic

They drove past a lake where
some fishermen were fishing.
Oh, oh! They seem to have
caught something!

While they were setting out the picnic, Rudolf Strudel, the famous aeroplane pilot, dropped by.

"Miss Honey!" he said, "A big thunderstorm is coming. You and the children must take shelter immediately!"

Everyone had been too busy putting out food to notice the black storm clouds gathering.

"Hurry!" Rudolf warned. "The rain will
start any minute."

C-r-a-a-a-a-c-c-k-k-k!
The lightning flashed! The thunder roared!
But everyone was safely inside the school bus.

No one got even the tiniest bit wet.
Not even Farmer Fox's tractor.
It was the best rainy-day picnic ever.

SPEEDBOAT SPIKE

Speedboat Spike
liked to take his
little boy, Swifty,
out for a ride
in his speedboat.

Oh, my! Didn't Spike think
he was the greatest!

Once he rammed a sailing boat.

Another time, he bumped
into a barge . . .

and knocked a lady's washing overboard.

e just wouldn't
down . . . .

. . . and he wouldn't stop bumping into things.

But that was before Officer Barnacle caught him . . . and made him stop!

Officer Barnacle ordered
Speedboat Spike to
keep his speedboat
in a paddling pool . . .
UP ON LAND!

Now Spike can go as fast as he likes,
without bumping into anyone.

But who is that
in the tiny little
speedboat?
Why, it's his little boy,
Swifty!

Oh dear! We are going
to need another paddling pool.

Go after him, Officer Barnacle!

SERGEANT MURPHY'S DAY

Sergeant Murphy was busy putting
parking tickets on cars when, suddenly

. . . who should come running out of the market
but Bananas Gorilla. He had stolen a bunch
of bananas and was trying to escape.

Huckle and Lowly Worm were watching.

Look, Murphy! He is stealing your motorcycle, too!

Sergeant Murphy was furiou[s]
Huckle said, "You may borr[ow]
my tricycle to chase after hi[m."]

Away they went,
chasing after
that naughty thief .

. . . through the crowded streets.

Don't YOU ever ride your tricycle in the street!

They crossed a drawbridge just as it
was opening to let a boat go through.

Well done, Sergeant Murphy!

Bananas stopped suddenly . . .

SPECIAL
TODAY

BANANA
SOUP

. . . and went into a restaurant.

Murphy said to Louie, who was the owner,
"I am looking for a thief!"

Together, they searched the whole restaurant, but they couldn't find Bananas anywhere.

Then Louie said, "Sit down and relax, Murphy. I will bring you and your friends something delicious to eat."

Louie brought them a bowl of banana soup.
Lowly said, "I'll bet Bananas Gorilla
would like to be here right now."

"Huckle, we mustn't forget to wash our
hands before eating," said Sergeant Murphy.
Lowly went along too.

When they came back, they discovered that their table had gone.

Indeed it was slowly creeping away when . . .

. . . it slipped on a banana skin!
And guess who was hiding underneath.

Sergeant Murphy, we are proud of you! Banana
must learn that it is naughty to steal things.

Carnival
An imprint of the Children's Division
of the Collins Publishing Group
8 Grafton Street, London W1X 3LA

Published by Carnival 1988

Copyright © Richard Scarry 1976

ISBN 0 00 194433 9

Printed & bound in Great Britain by
PURNELL BOOK PRODUCTION LIMITED
A MEMBER OF BPCC plc